An I Can Read Book™

Elvis the Rooster
Almost Goes to Heaven

Dennis Cazet

HarperCollins*Publishers*

For the Vosti chicks

HarperCollins®, 🐭®, and I Can Read Book® are
trademarks of HarperCollins Publishers Inc.

Elvis the Rooster Almost Goes to Heaven
Copyright © 2003 by Denys Cazet
Printed in the U.S.A. All rights reserved.
www.harperchildrens.com

Library of Congress Cataloging-in-Publication Data
Cazet, Denys.
  Elvis the rooster almost goes to heaven / Denys Cazet.
    p. cm. — (I can read book)
  Summary: Elvis the rooster thinks he has died when he fails
to crow the rising of the sun but the chickens find a way to
restore his pluck.
  ISBN 0-06-000500-9 — ISBN 0-06-000501-7 (lib. bdg.)
  [1. Roosters—Fiction. 2. Chickens—Fiction. 3. Humorous
stories.] I. Title. II. Series.
PZ7.C2985El 2003   2002014416
[Fic]—dc21   CIP
                                                   AC

1 2 3 4 5 6 7 8 9 10
❖
First Edition

1: Elvis Lost

Elvis strutted

to the edge of the barn roof.

He was a proud rooster.

Proud to be so good-looking.

Proud to be loved by so many.

Proud to wake the world.

Elvis waited.

Then, there it was.

A thin bit of light in the east.

It was time to lift the sun.

It was time to crow.

Elvis took a deep breath.

Suddenly, a bug

flew into his mouth.

"ACK!" he gasped.

The sun began to rise.

"ACK! ACK!"

The sun rose higher.

"ACK! ACK! ACK!"

Elvis swallowed the bug.

He gasped.

He saw the sun in the morning sky.

Elvis saw the farm animals waking.

"It can't be," he moaned.

But it was.

The sun had risen without him.

Elvis fainted.

2: Elvis Found

Little Willie and Rocky
listened to the chickens.
"So," said Little Willie,
"Elvis is missing."
"Yes," said Daniela.
"Please help us find him.
He's been gone all day."

11

"Something's happened," said Gina.

"He's never late for breakfast!"

"Or lunch," added Lia.

"When was the last time
you saw him?" asked Little Willie.
"This morning, when he went out
to bring the sun up," said Daniela.

Little Willie looked at Rocky.

He pointed at the barn.

"Check the roof," he said.

Rocky shrugged. "You're the boss."

Rocky climbed up a ladder

and looked around.

He saw Elvis leaning

against the weather vane.

"Worthless," muttered Elvis.

"I might as well be a cow."

15

"He's here," shouted Rocky.

"The sun came up without me," moaned Elvis. "I'm no good anymore."

"Is he alive?" shouted Little Willie.

"Sort of," said Rocky.

3: Heaven?

Rocky picked up Elvis.

He carried him into the coop.

"The sun came up without him,"

he said.

"Lay him on the bed,"

said Little Willie.

Elvis's eyes fluttered open.

17

"Is this heaven?" Elvis asked weakly.

"It looks like a chicken coop."

"It is a chicken coop," said Little Willie.

"Your chicken coop."

"I'm not dead?" Elvis asked.

"Not yet," said Rocky.

"Too bad." Elvis sighed.

"What good is living

if you're not a rooster anymore?"

"Elvis," said Little Willie,

"you're still a rooster.

Every rooster has to do his share.

The sun is big and heavy.

It takes more than one rooster

to make the sun come up."

"I'm going fast," said Elvis.

He reached out to the chickens.

"Good-bye, girls," he whispered.

4: Elvis Fades

Little Willie looked at Elvis.

"He's lost his pluck," he said.

"Cluck?" said Lia.

"He's lost his cluck?"

"Pluck!" said Little Willie. "Pluck!"

"Duck?" said Elvis, sitting up.

"You're giving my job to a duck?"

21

"Ducks can't crow," said Gina.

"Pluck," said Daniela. "His spirit.

His belief in himself!"

Elvis flopped back onto the bed.

"It's getting darker," he moaned.

Rocky turned on the light.

"OH!" gasped Elvis. "See?

The sun came up without me again!"

23

Rocky turned off the lights.

The room was dark.

Elvis sat up.

"Night already?" he said.

Rocky turned on the lights.

"Gee," said Elvis sadly.

"The days and nights come and go
so quickly in the end."

"Hmmm," muttered Little Willie.
"I have an idea. Meet me outside."

5: Pluck

After Little Willie told everyone

his plan to help Elvis,

they met in the chicken yard.

"Daniela, did you get the flashlight?"

"Got it!" said Daniela.

"Here's the ladder," said Rocky.

Little Willie wiggled the ladder.

"It doesn't look safe," he said.

"I found it in the barn," Rocky said.

"It will have to do," said Little Willie.

"We don't have much time

before morning.

Do we all understand the plan?"

"Get Elvis's cluck back," said Lia.

"Pluck," said Daniela.

"Truck?" said Gina.

"I didn't even know he could drive."

"PLUCK!" said Daniela. "PLUCK!"

"Please, girls," said Little Willie.

"I'll say it again.

I want you to stand on the ladder

outside the coop window.

When Elvis gets up,

turn on the flashlight.

He'll think it's the sun.

When he sits down, lower it."

"I don't get it," said Gina.

Lia rolled her eyes.

"We're trying to get

Elvis's cluck back," she said.

"PLUCK!" said Daniela.

"I still don't get it," said Gina.

32

6: The Sun Visits Elvis

Little Willie and Rocky

went back into the coop.

Elvis was snoring.

A light went on outside the window.

"Sun's coming up," said Little Willie.

Elvis opened his eyes.

He sat up.

The light went higher.

"Did you see that?" Elvis asked.

He stood up.

The light went higher.

"The sun is following me," said Elvis.

He stood on the bed.

The light went higher.

It began to teeter back and forth.

"What's the matter with the sun?"

Elvis asked.

"Help!" someone yelled.

There was a loud snap

and something crashed.

The light tumbled by the window

and disappeared.

7: The Sun Goes Out

Elvis rushed to the window.

"The sun fell out of the sky!" he said.

Little Willie scratched his head.

"Well," he said. "You can see

that no matter how the sun tries,

it can't stay up without your help."

Elvis nodded.

"I heard it," said Elvis.

"I heard the sun shout 'help!'"

Daniela staggered into the coop.

Lia and Gina limped in behind her.

Elvis looked at the chickens.

"The sun called out to me," he said.

"Look, Elvis," said Little Willie,

"there's only one thing

that can help the sun.

And that's the crow of a young,

good-looking, strong . . ."

Elvis held up his wing.

"I know who you're talking about,"

he said. "It's me, isn't it?"

Little Willie nodded.

"All right," said Elvis, pointing

at the chickens. "I'll do it for them."

8: Elvis Does It

Everyone climbed up to the roof.

Daniela led Elvis to the edge.

"You can do it," she said.

Elvis looked across the dark hills.

Then, there it was.

A thread of light in the east.

It was time.

Elvis took a deep breath.

Suddenly,

a big beetle flew into his mouth.

"ACK!" he gasped. "ACK! ACK!"

"Crow," shouted Little Willie.

"Crow!" yelled Rocky.

Light began to creep into the sky.

Daniela wrapped her wings around Elvis and jerked him tightly. The beetle shot out of his mouth. Elvis gasped.

He crowed.

The sun rose.

He crowed again.

The sun rose higher.

He crowed until the sun was behind the old oak tree on the hill.

"Am I good, or what?" Elvis said.

The roosters climbed down.

The three chickens sat on the roof.

They looked down on the farm.

"Well . . . we did it!" said Daniela.

"We found Elvis's cluck," said Lia.

"Pluck!" said Daniela.

"We found Elvis's pluck!"

"We did?" asked Gina. "Where?"

DATE DUE

DE 30 03			
MY 1 0 '04			
JE 02 '04			
JE 22 '04			
AG 18 04			
OC 26 04			
'05			
05			
JE 30 06			
AG 23 06			
JE 1 9 08			